There's a Cow in the Cabbage Patch

Clare Beaton

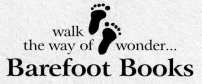

walk
the way of wonder...
Barefoot Books

There's a cow in the cabbage patch, moo, moo, moo!

She should be in the dairy, what shall we do?

There's a dove in the dairy, coo, coo, coo!

He should be in the birdhouse, what shall we do?

There's an owl in the birdhouse, t-wit, t-wit, t-woo!

He should be in the old barn, what shall we do?

There's a horse in the old barn, and a donkey, too!

They should be in the stable, what shall we do?

There's a rooster in the stable, cock-a-doodle-doo!

He should be in the henhouse, what shall we do?

There's a pig in the henhouse, with piglets pink and new.

They should be in the pigsty, what shall we do?

There's a black sheep in the pigsty, with lambs one and two.

They should be in the meadow, what shall we do?

dairy

henhouse

stabl

barn

meadow

pigsty

birdhouse

**Tell them all it's dinnertime, then it won't be long
'til all these naughty animals are back where they belong!**

Praise for Clare Beaton

How Big is a Pig?
"Bold, bright tableaux...a sassy, unexpected wrap-up; Beaton will have her audience's attention all sewn up" — *Publishers Weekly*

Mother Goose Remembers
"Beaton's splendid collages revel in the whimsy of Mother Goose. The artwork is executed with Beaton's signature flair" — Starred *Kirkus Review*

Mother Goose Remembers
"She exquisitely and inventively crafts each picture" — *Publishers Weekly*

One Moose, Twenty Mice
"Young viewers will find the fuzzy menagerie endearing, and they'll giggle through the rollicking kitty hunt" — *Bulletin of the Center for Children's Books*

Zoë and her Zebra
"A visually tactile phantasmagoria...the illustrations beg to be touched" — *School Library Journal*

For Annabel and Benedict – S. B.
For Gavin, who is frightened of cows – C. B.

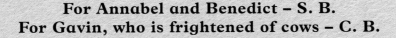

Barefoot Books
37 West 17th Street
4th Floor East
New York, New York 10011

Text copyright © 2001 by Stella Blackstone Illustrations copyright © 2001 by Clare Beaton
The moral right of Stella Blackstone to be identified as the author and Clare Beaton
to be identified as the illustrator of this work has been asserted
First published in the United States of America in 2001 by Barefoot Books, Inc.
All rights reserved No part of this book may be reproduced in any form or by any means,
electronic or mechanical, including photocopying, recording, or by any information storage
and retrieval system, without permission in writing from the publisher
This book is printed on 100% acid-free paper This book was typeset in Plantin Schoolbook Bold
20 on 28 point The illustrations were prepared in felt with beads and buttons
Graphic design by Judy Linard, England Color transparencies by Jonathan Fisher
Photography, England Color separation by Grafiscan, Italy
Printed and bound in Singapore by Tien Wah Press (Pte.) Ltd.

1 3 5 7 9 8 6 4 2

U.S. Cataloging-in-Publication Data
(Library of Congress Standards)

Beaton, Clare.
    There's a cow in the cabbage patch / Clare Beaton [ill.] ; [text by Stella Blackstone]- Colophon. - 1st ed.
[32] p. : col. ill. ; cm.
Summary: All the animals in this mixed-up farmyard are out of place, but when dinnertime
comes around, suddenly they are all back where they belong.
ISBN 1-84148-333-8
1. Domestic animals. 2. Stories in rhyme. I. Blackstone, Stella. II. Title.
[E] 21 2001 AC CIP